Noisy Birds

Ryan and Raquel Underwood

ISBN-13: 978-1530195657
ISBN: 1530195659

Quail

Listen to the noisy birds.

That's a pretend bird.

9

Hummingbird

(flutter flutter)

That's a quiet bird.

That's a *really* quiet bird.

That bird is too loud!

23

What bird makes that noise?

A silly bird!

Made in the USA
Middletown, DE
30 January 2021